PONY CAMP diaries

Cassie and Charm

For Katie J, with thanks xx

tiger tales

5 River Road, Suite 128, Wilton, CT 06897
Published in the United States 2019
Originally published in Great Britain in 2007
by the Little Tiger Group
Text copyright © 2007, 2019 Kelly McKain
Illustrations copyright © 2007, 2019 Mandy Stanley
ISBN-13: 978-1-68010-442-4
ISBN-10: 1-68010-442-X
Printed in China
STP/1800/0251/0219
10 9 8 7 6 5 4 3 2 1

For more insight and activities, visit us at www.tigertalesbooks.com

PONY CAMP
diaries

Cassie and Charm

by Kelly McKain

Illustrated by Mandy Stanley

tiger tales

Other titles in the series:

Megan and Mischief

Penny and Prince

Chloe and Cookie

Sophie and Sparkle

Emily and Emerald

THIS DIARY BELONGS TO

Cassie

Contents

Dear Riders,

A warm welcome to Sunnyside Stables!

Sunnyside is our home, and for the next week it will be yours, too! We're a big family—my husband, Jason, and I have two children, Olivia and Tyler, plus two dogs ... and all the ponies, of course!

We have friendly yard staff and a very talented instructor, Sally, to help you get the most out of your week. If you have any worries or questions about anything at all, just ask. We're here to help, and we want your vacation to be as enjoyable as possible—so don't be shy!

As you know, you will have a pony to take care of as your own for the week. Your pony can't wait to meet you and start having fun! During your stay, you'll be caring for your pony, improving your riding, enjoying long rides in the country, learning new skills (this week we have a special surprise for our more experienced riders!), and making new friends.

We'll also be off to the beach for a day of fun with our ponies—just imagine cantering along the sandy shore together! Add swimming, games, movies, barbecues, and a gymkhana, and you're in for a fun-filled vacation to remember!

This special Pony Camp Diary is for you to fill with all your vacation memories. We hope you'll write all about your adventures here at Sunnyside Stables—because we know you're going to have a lot of them!

Wishing you a wonderful time with us!

Jess xx

Sunnyside Stables

stables
x 4

hay barn

feed room

Stables
x 4

Barn

ME on Charm

To upper
fields →

Monday, after lunch

Well, here I am at Pony Camp, and Jess has given me this special diary to write all about it!

It's amazing here, with so many ponies and two manèges and a swimming pool! And the girls are really nice, too. I just wish that Apple was here to enjoy it with me. She's my pony … well, I mean, she was my pony, but I got too big to ride her, and Mom and Dad said they had to sell her. That was 1 month, 23 days and, um, 5 hours ago. And I haven't ridden since—well, I hadn't until this morning, anyway. I found it really strange being on a pony again, and I was sad that it wasn't Apple.

When I got here, other cars were pulling up. Girls tumbled out, chattering excitedly and dragging big suitcases into the farmhouse.

I was feeling nervous, so I stayed close to Mom when she went to register me in the office. I wish I hadn't, though, because she was doing that annoying thing of talking about me as if I'm not there, saying "Cassie" this and "she" that.

She was telling Sally the instructor and Lydia (one of the stable girls) about me not riding since they sold Apple. Well, actually, she said, "since we sold Apple," and I said, "since you did" because I had nothing to do with it—I would never have given up my beautiful pony! Then she said how I won't even go back to the stables where I used to keep Apple, and how I've lost touch with my riding friends because I always said no to going up there with them and after a while they stopped asking me.

I was getting really upset and annoyed, and

♘ Cassie and Charm ♘

I think Sally noticed 'cos she sent me off into the farmhouse to unpack and meet the other girls. Lydia walked up there with me, and on the way, she squeezed my shoulders and said, "Don't worry, Cassie—you'll be okay at Sunnyside." That was so nice of her, but it also almost made me start crying.

When I got to the room. I started unpacking right away to take my mind off Apple. I could hear girls chatting in the other rooms, but mine was empty. The bed by the  window was unmade and covered in clothes and magazines, but the bunk beds looked free, so I took the top one.

After a few minutes, Mom came up to say good-bye because she had to go to work. She and Dad are always really busy at their offices, and my big brother, Henry, is away this week, too, on a hiking trip with some friends. He loves canoeing over waterfalls and stuff like that. I used to be outdoorsy, too, and I practically lived at the stables while Apple was there! But when she was sold, I ended up moping around in my room, not really knowing what to do with myself. Mom and Dad tried to talk to me about getting a new pony, but I was so upset I couldn't even think about it. In the end, Mom booked me on this vacation to try and cheer me up. That was only a couple of weeks ago, and she kept saying how lucky I was to get the last spot.

I tried to tell her that I didn't feel like riding, but she did that thing she does where she acts as if she's at work and bosses me around, saying things like, "Come on, darling, don't be silly about this, it'll be good for you."

16

Why can't she just see that I miss Apple so much it hurts? She wasn't just a pony to ride; she was my best friend!

I went down to wave to Mom, and when I got back upstairs, there was a girl sitting on the bottom bunk cuddling a really tattered toy rabbit. When I came in she stuffed it under her pillow, but I got Frieda the frog out of my suitcase, where I'd been hiding her.

The girl smiled and climbed up to sit on my bunk, bringing her rabbit with her. "Are you here on your own, too?" she asked.

She was relieved when I said that I was. She'd been worried that everyone would have friends here already.

Her name is Skye (and her rabbit is named

Sniff) and she's nine, like me. She's from Denver, which is kind of on the way back to my hometown from here. She has beautiful long, dark hair with some little braids and beads in it, and she's wearing a really cool pink tie-dye top. When I asked where she got it from, she said she'd dyed it herself! I'm going to try dying a couple of my T-shirts when I get home.

Skye

Sni

Then Olivia, Jess's daughter, came bursting in (turns out she's the owner of the messy bed by the window!). She climbed up on my bunk, too, and soon we were all chatting about what riding and stuff we'd done.

Me   Olivia   Skye

When Olivia told us she had her own pony, I ended

up admitting that I used to have one. I wasn't planning to tell anyone about Apple in case I got upset, but it just came out. Skye said she could imagine how I felt—her mom gave her cat away because of her baby brother being allergic to it. And Olivia said how she couldn't even bear to imagine selling her pony, Tally. I'm so relieved they don't think I'm spoiled for being upset when I've been lucky enough to have had my own pony in the first place. It's great knowing they understand.

Jess came up and sent us down to the yard just then. The other girls were there, and Sally and Lydia, and we had to go around in a circle and say our names and where we're from.

Lydia

Sally

In the older girls' room there are:

Ricosha

Tanika

Jordan

Ricosha and Tanika are both 12 and they've come together from Carroll. Jordan is 11 and she's really giggly and silly, and she says she's always getting in trouble at school for talking during class!

The girls in the younger room are:

Yasmine

Ruby

Molly

Yasmine is from Hillside, and Ruby and Molly have come together and live nearby. They're all eight.

Sally gave us these schedules so we can see roughly what we're doing each day, although she says it will change sometimes. In fact, it changed right away 'cos then we had a tour around the yard instead of a Pony Care lecture.

Pony Camp Schedule

8 a.m.: Wake up, get dressed, have breakfast
8:45 a.m.: Help in the yard, bring in the ponies from field, muck out stables, do feeds, etc.
9:30 a.m.: Prepare ponies for morning lessons (quick groom, tack up, etc.)
10 a.m.: Morning riding lesson
11 a.m.: Morning break—milk and cookies
11:20 a.m.: Pony Care lecture
12:30 p.m.: Lunch and free time
2 p.m.: Afternoon riding lesson
3 p.m.: Break—milk and cookies
3:20 p.m.: Pony Care lecture
4:30 p.m.: Jobs around the yard (i.e., cleaning tack, sweeping up, mixing evening feeds, turning out ponies)
5:30 p.m.: Free time before dinner
6 p.m.: Dinner (and cleaning up!)
7 p.m.: Evening activity
8:30 p.m.: Showers and hot chocolate
9:30 p.m.: Lights out and NO TALKING!

Sally showed us around Sunnyside and
we all went **WOW!** when we saw the
swimming pool and the game room. Then
she took us into the main barn, where all the
ponies who live outside in the summer were
waiting for us. Lydia was busy tacking them up
and getting them ready for our lesson and the
other girls got really excited, wondering which
ponies they were going to get and saying how
cute they looked.

The barn smelled exactly like the one in my
old yard, and without thinking I began looking
for Apple among the ponies. With a start I
realized what I was doing. That barn smell
made me miss her
so much! I was
really relieved
when we left to
go to the fire drill
meeting point.

Sally also went over some other safety things, like:

1. How to tie a pony up properly.

2. How important it is to put all the equipment away and not leave things lying around.

3. How you must always tell someone where you're going if you leave the group, even if it's just to go to the bathroom or to get a different grooming brush from the tack room.

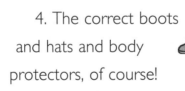

4. The correct boots and hats and body protectors, of course!

Then we all had to practice tying slip knots in our lead ropes. Molly was having trouble, so I did hers, and then I did Ruby's, too, because she was looking a little bit confused. I'd tied up Apple so many times that I can do it with my eyes closed, so it was no big deal.

Then it was time to meet our ponies. We picked up our hats and gloves and went out into the yard. Secretly, I felt really sick.

Sally said, "You'll each have your own pony for the entire week. You'll feed, groom, and take care of him or her in addition to riding."

Everyone was grinning, and Ricosha and Tanika were actually jumping up and down with excitement, but I didn't feel that way at all. I didn't want a new pony to take care of, even just for a week. I only wanted Apple.

It was great to see Skye so happy, though. She got a beautiful bay Arab cross named Fisher, with a shiny, tumbling mane that's a bit like her own hair! They just seem to fit together, like me and Apple used to. Jordan got a palomino named Mischief, and she made us all laugh by saying, "Sounds like he's just perfect for me! That's what Mom would say, anyway … and my teachers!"

Molly was so excited about getting Sugar that it took forever to persuade her to stop making a fuss over him and mount up!

I kept myself busy by helping out with the other girls' stirrups, hoping that Sally wouldn't notice me. But when I turned around, she was standing there with a gray Connemara. "Cassie, meet Charm," she said with a smile. "He's a handsome boy, and he'll definitely cheer you up. Plus, he's a great jumper." She winked at me and added, "And you'll find out why that matters later on."

Charm

I forced myself to smile back and took the reins. I fussed over Charm, but only because Sally was watching. Inside, I missed Apple so much I felt like crying. But I took some deep breaths and managed to hold the tears in—I don't want the girls thinking I'm a spoiled brat or something.

So, this is who everyone got in the end:

Me + Charm

Ricosha + Flame

Tanika + Sparkle

Olivia + Tally

Ruby + Cookie

Yasmine + Prince

Skye + Fisher

Molly + Sugar

Jordan + Mischief
(like her!)

I still didn't feel like riding, but I couldn't
exactly say anything in front of everyone else,
could I? So I got on, and it felt really strange
because I was much higher off the ground
than I was on Apple. Also, Charm is slimmer
than she was, so my legs were in a totally
different position. I kept readjusting my stirrups,
but I couldn't seem to find a leg position that
felt right.

Still, even if I'm not really into the riding,
the other girls are so nice I think I'll have a
fun week. Like, it was so funny when Mischief
wandered away from the mounting block,
leaving Jordan standing there giggling with her
leg in the air! We all laughed at that, except

Sally, of course, who said, "Don't encourage him!" and made him back up and stand still while Jordan got herself straightened out.

For our first lesson, we all rode together so that Sally could assess which group to put us in. As we walked our ponies up to the manège, the other girls kept saying how handsome Charm was, but all I could think about was Apple. I started getting upset, but luckily Sally asked me to lead everyone into the manège, so I had to think about steering Charm through the gate and onto the track.

It was so strange riding another pony after Apple. As we trotted on, Charm was going around with his nose poking out. (Apple used to always get nicely on the bit once we'd warmed up.) I shortened my reins to try and pull him in,

but that didn't seem to work. Sally called out,
"Relax your shoulders and get your elbows
back, Cassie. Charm is feeling your tension, and
it's making him resist you."

I wanted to say, *It's not my fault he's not
paying attention to me.* But, of course, I didn't. I
just looked ahead and tried to relax more. We
made a few transitions from walk and trot to
halt, and Sally called out to all of us, "I said
forward to halt, which doesn't mean just sitting
there and letting your ponies run out of
steam!" Oh, dear! But at least I wasn't the
only one getting corrected.

Then we did a bunch of changes of
direction and circles, and Sally got a few
different people to lead. That was easier for
me because then Charm could just follow the
pony in front, and I didn't have to keep nagging
at him. But when it was my turn to trot a
circle, I had to use my legs a lot to even get

him off the track! And when we cantered to the back of the ride (you could choose if you wanted to or not), it took me two corners to get a canter. That was a shock—I only ever had to sit down and touch Apple with my outside leg, and she'd whoosh right off.

At lunchtime I sat with my two roommates, and Olivia told us what it's like living at the stables all the time. It sounds amazing! I wish I lived somewhere like this—if I did, there would have been plenty of space to keep Apple, and she could have stayed with me forever.

♘ Cassie and Charm ♘

When we were helping to clean up after lunch, Ricosha and Tanika showed us this singing and dancing routine they've been working on. Me, Olivia, Skye, and Jordan tried to learn some of it. We weren't exactly very good, and we all kept bursting into giggles! It was so much fun, and it felt like being back with the girls at my old stable yard before I stopped going. It made me really miss them.

Then Sally came in and read out the names for the groups, and would you believe this is the exact thing she said?

Cassie, I've put you in Group B because of all your experience, but you need to stay focused and pay attention, or I might decide to move you to Group A where you can have more opportunity to focus on your partnership with Charm.

I was just *staring* at her then, probably with my mouth hanging wide open.

I couldn't believe it; I'd almost ended up in the *beginners'* group! Me and Apple used to ride in the *advanced* lessons at my stables! I couldn't help feeling annoyed with Charm for not listening to me. He really made me look bad in the assessment!

It's strange that he's being so naughty when Sally keeps saying how great he is. Oh! I just had a secret thought. What if it's just that he doesn't like *me*?

On my bunk bed after dinner, chilling out!

This afternoon we had our first Pony Care lecture, which was all about tack, and Lydia showed us how to tack up on Yasmine's cute piebald, Prince. I knew how, 'cos of Apple, but the younger ones hadn't ever done it on their own, and even Jordan wasn't sure about whether the noseband went under or over the cheek pieces. Lydia explained about some of the different bits and nosebands and what they're for. Then she pointed to parts of the saddle, and we had to call out what they were.

They are:

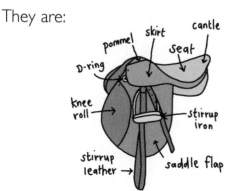

Then we had to try tacking up for ourselves.
I helped Jordan check Mischief's saddle when
she wasn't sure if it was in the right place, then
I put the bits in for Ruby and Molly because
they hadn't done it before, and I was worried
they might trap their fingers. I was about to
help Skye pick out Fisher's feet (in case he
stepped on her toes) when Lydia came over
to me and said I needed to get going with
tacking up Charm or we wouldn't be ready
in time for the lesson. I told her it was fine
'cos I'm quick at it, but she said, "I didn't really
mean that, Cassie. It's about spending time
with your pony. You can always give
him a good brushing, too."

So I tacked Charm up in about two minutes
because he didn't look like he needed a
brush to me. I didn't know what to do
after that, so I just fiddled with my
boot until everyone was ready,

pretending that I'd gotten a stone down it.

After the lesson this afternoon, I definitely think I'm right about Charm not liking me! It's not that he bucked me off or anything, but he didn't even try to do things correctly. I just couldn't seem to get any impulsion, so I had to flap around to make a transition, and he kept trying to put his head down and yank the reins out of my hands as though he didn't want me riding him. Sally told me to relax again and a couple of times she got annoyed because my mind wandered off and I didn't hear her instructions. Of course, it was because I was thinking of Apple and how much fun we'd be having if she'd come on this vacation with me.

Mischief was being playful in the lesson, cutting off the corners, and Sally said Jordan had to stop finding it funny and concentrate on keeping

Silly Mischief!

her inside leg on, so at least I wasn't the only one having problems.

There was one good thing, though—a very exciting thing, actually! After the lesson, Sally called us all into the middle and announced that she'll be taking a few of us out onto the cross-country course! That was the special surprise Jess mentioned in her welcome letter! Sally also told us we'll be having a mini cross-country competition on Friday when all the parents are here!

I've always wanted to try cross country, ever since our stables went on this day trip to the Horse Trials. It was totally amazing watching the horses leap over these giant fences right in front of you! I've taken Apple over the

odd log or low hedge on a hack out and even
that was really exciting, so I can't wait!

After Sally had made the announcement,
she smiled at me and added, "That's
why I said you're lucky you've
got Charm, Cassie, because
he's such a great jumper!"

I made myself smile back, but
all I could think of was how much
Apple would've loved jumping an entire course
and how we never got the chance to try it.

Skye was really unsure about trying, and
Sally promised her that no one has to do
anything she doesn't want to here at Pony
Camp. "It's no problem if you want to join
in with Group A while we go out on the
course," she told her, then said to us all, "and
if I don't feel that some of you are ready to
tackle cross country, I'll ask you to join the
other group."

Ricosha and Tanika gave each other a worried look then, because they weren't sure Sally would think they were ready. She's going to decide who's allowed to do it after tomorrow morning's lesson, and I really hope she will let them join in. It'll be way more fun if we can all do it together.

Oh, gotta go now. Ricosha's saying that today's dishes are done (we're taking turns—I'm on dish-washing duty with Skye on Wednesday), and Olivia and Skye have just come in to change 'cos we're all going swimming!

I'm snuggled up in bed with Frieda—writing this by flashlight!

Swimming was really fun and so was running back through the house in our towels, doing giant leaps to try not to make too many wet footprints. Then we took showers, and Jess helped us dry our hair and made us all hot chocolate in the kitchen.

Olivia and Skye are both asleep now, but we were all whispering for a long time after lights out. Skye is still worried about doing the cross country, and Olivia was trying to tell her how great she did in the lesson this afternoon. I said something about how Skye shouldn't worry because she'll easily manage the course, and suddenly everything seemed to go wrong.

"Well, I'm sorry I'm not as confident as you, Cassie!" she said in a grumbly voice, and then got up and marched off to the bathroom.

"Good job, Cassie," Olivia whispered.

"What did I say?" I hissed. "I only meant she's a really good rider."

"Well, you said, 'Don't be so silly! It's easy-peasy!' like she's silly for worrying."

My stomach flipped over, and I felt my face go burning hot. Had I really said that? "I didn't mean it that way," I insisted.

When Skye came back, I said I was sorry about my words coming out wrong, and how I'd only meant it like she's a really good rider.

Luckily, she was okay about it—phew! She's still not sure about doing the cross country, but she's going to think about it at least.

Good night!

♘ Cassie and Charm ♘

Tuesday—I'm quickly writing this before we get called down for lunch

Well, now I know for sure that Charm doesn't like me.

In our lesson we were working on the skills we'll need for the cross country. Me and Charm started off okay-ish, but when we were all practicing our jumping position down the long side, he took advantage of me not having as much control as usual and kept veering off the track on purpose. I was trying really hard, but he just wouldn't listen to me.

Sally didn't see it like that, though. I wish she didn't think Charm was so perfect, because then she might stop blaming me for his mistakes. She called out, "Cassie, the more annoyed you get, the less Charm is going to cooperate with you because he senses your tension. Breathe out, sit deep in the saddle, and relax your arms and shoulders."

I did it, but I felt embarrassed with everyone watching.

"That's better," she said. "Now, start again." I tried to stay relaxed, but I still felt upset after the lesson. Maybe that's why an awful thing happened in the Pony Care lecture. Something else came out of my mouth all wrong, like it did to Skye last night. Only this time it was to Jordan.

I wasn't going to write this down, but I can't seem to get it out of my head. We were learning about grooming, standing in the barn with our ponies, copying what Lydia was showing us on Sparkle. As we were doing circles with our rubber curry combs, she said something like, "A good partnership in the manège or on the cross-country course starts right here, girls.

♡ Cassie and Charm ♡

Spending time with your pony, talking to him or her, grooming and caring, all lay the foundations for your partnership while riding."

Before she said that, I'd thought I was just brushing a pony, but then suddenly it felt like I was being disloyal to Apple. Jordan was next to me, and she was cooing all over Mischief, telling him how handsome he was while she gently wiped his eyes with the special blue sponges in his grooming kit. I tried to ignore it, but she kept going on and on and on.

Handsome!

Then I started imagining Apple having her eyes wiped by Laura, her new owner, and I wondered if she's completely forgotten about me already. That made me feel really upset and that's when Jordan said, "Cassie, can I borrow your curry comb when you're finished? Mischief's seems to be missing from his kit."

Before I could stop myself, I snapped, "No, you can't!"

Jordan just blinked at me in shock, her usual grin gone. I could feel my cheeks burning with embarrassment. I still can't believe I said that!

I didn't know what to do then, so I went around the other side of Charm where Jordan couldn't see me. After the lecture, I wanted to say I was sorry to her, but she walked off really fast, arm in arm with Skye, and now she won't look me in the eye.

Oh, dear! Things just don't seem to be going very well for me at all.

At least I've got the cross country to look forward to. We're walking the course tomorrow, and then going out on our ponies for a practice run. I'm really excited to see what jumps we'll be doing and how high they are.

Gotta go—Jess is calling that lunch is ready.

I can't believe what just happened!

My hand's shaking so much I can hardly write. Sally hasn't chosen me to do the cross country!

And even worse, everyone else in our group is doing it!

I feel so silly. I just assumed I'd be taking part, and instead I'll have to go with the beginners tomorrow. I don't understand. I'm about the most experienced rider here, with Olivia and Jordan, anyway. I can easily manage a few cross-country fences!

Sally came in just when we were finishing lunch and made the announcement. I was sure there'd been a mistake, so I hurried out after her. "Did you just say I'm not doing the cross country?" I asked.

"Yes," she said, and kept on walking.

"But why?" I gasped.

"Because I'm the instructor, and I don't think you're ready," she told me, still walking.

But I wouldn't give up. "Skye's allowed, and she's not that experienced or confident!"

Sally sighed and said, "You haven't been putting the effort in, Cassie. You're not focused enough."

"But I'm one of the best riders here," I argued.

"It's not just about technical ability," she said. "Riding is about being a team with your pony. Cross country can be dangerous, and you need to have a good partnership."

Huh! How unfair is that?!

"But that's Charm's fault," I insisted. "He doesn't listen to me. He'd be better in a flash or drop noseband and a stronger bit...."

Sally stopped in her tracks and looked

me straight in the eye. I suddenly realized I was talking back to an instructor, and I felt a little scared. "Cassie, the problem is not your pony," she said sharply. "I know Charm. He's got a wonderful nature, and he's very well mannered."

"But…," I began.

"Cassie," she said again, cutting me off. "The problem is you."

I stood there feeling stunned as she marched into the office. Why doesn't she understand? Can't she see what Charm is really like?

So that's why I've been hiding behind the back of the feed barn ever since, writing this and trying not to cry.

I wish I could just go home.

Oh, no—Olivia's calling me. I guess I'd better get back to the yard.

We just finished up in the yard— I found a little space in the tack room to sit and write in here

Oh, dear! This afternoon didn't go very well, either. In fact, everything seems to be going more and more wrong for me!

I was too embarrassed to look at Sally after what happened at lunchtime, and I was so annoyed with Charm for making me miss out on the cross country that I felt really tense and couldn't seem to control him at all.

ME
Seesawing!

He wouldn't go into canter, so I started seesawing back and forth to try and make him. Sally called out, "You're tensing up as you go into the corner and letting his nose poke out, Cassie. He's not collected, and he has no impulsion. Shorten up your reins, sit deep into your saddle, relax your arms, and keep your leg on rather than kicking like that!" She said it in a fed-up way like it was the millionth time she'd told me. I did try, but it just didn't work. I mean, I know how I should do it—it's not my fault Charm ignores me!

Mischief was playing around, too, but after a few times when he cut off the corner, Jordan got him into a perfect canter. I was so busy feeling frustrated about Charm's behavior that by the time I realized everyone was cheering for Jordan, they'd stopped. Then Sally made it worse by saying, "Please don't sulk, Cassie; you can do as well as that if you put your mind to it." So then everyone thought I hadn't cheered on purpose! They all looked at me, and I got completely red and flustered.

Then in the Pony Care lecture on feeding, it was awful 'cos we had to get into pairs— Ricosha and Tanika went together, and Olivia and Yasmine, and Ruby and Molly, and Skye and Jordan, and I was left with no one. Lydia said, "Cassie, just make a three, that's fine,"

 but as I looked around, no one smiled at me or invited me to join them. I went with Olivia and Yasmine in the end, but I don't think Yas exactly wanted me there.

We had to make up feeds for horses who do different amounts of work, and Yas didn't seem to have any ideas, even though Olivia tried to help her think. Then Jess called Olivia in to do her math homework. Yas still wasn't saying anything, and in the end we got so behind the others that I just had to fill in the entire sheet myself.

I'd better go in now, before I get into trouble for not telling anyone where I am.

Still Tuesday

It's 11:34 p.m., but I'm still awake because I've been having a whispery chat with Olivia. I was crying, so she came to sit on my bunk, and we ended up talking for a long time. I'm so upset because, well, to explain it correctly, I'll have to start from the beginning.

This evening, we all went outside to play games like limbo and stuck in the mud. It was really fun, but when Jordan and Tanika were picking teams for volleyball, I ended up being picked last and just standing there on my own. There were four on each team, and Jordan said, "It's okay, you can have Cassie," so I went on Tan's team.

I thought Jordan only said that to be nice to the other team. But then afterward, when we were going inside, I went to put the colored bands back into the game

room, and when I came out I saw Jordan and
Skye huddled together in the hallway. Jordan
whispered, "I so didn't want Cassie on

our team. She's such a spoiled
brat. I can't believe she wouldn't
even lend me her curry comb,
or say good job when I finally
got Mischief around that corner.

And Yas says she was too scared of
her to suggest anything when they were doing
the feeds thing! And she totally took over
when Molly and Ruby were tacking up!"

I ducked back behind the door, my stomach
churning—why didn't they realize I was only
trying to help the younger girls? And I only did
all the feed questions myself because Yasmine
didn't have any ideas! I hoped Skye would stick
up for me, but then I heard her say, "She was
mean to me, too, about the cross country."

I almost leaped out and cried, "But I said

I was sorry and you said it was okay!" but I
made myself stay where I was. My heart was
hammering so hard, I was sure they'd hear it.

"She's a nightmare!" Jordan said then. "I
mean, if she doesn't want to be here, why did
she come? She's spoiling it for everyone else!"

As they walked off, I stayed frozen to the
spot, my legs trembling. I felt really sick hearing
them talk about me like that.

Because suddenly I saw everything
differently.

And I knew they were right.

I hung around in the game room for a long time by myself, and then Jess came and sent me upstairs, saying it was almost time for lights out. I got ready quickly and jumped into bed before anyone could say anything. Skye was already asleep, even though the light was still on. Jess said good night and once it was dark, I tried to go to sleep, too, but I couldn't stop thinking about what they'd said. The tears I'd been bottling up inside since I got here just started pouring out, and I couldn't stop them.

That's when Olivia crept up to my bunk.

I was all sniffly and I kept bursting into more tears, but I managed to tell her what Jordan and Skye had said about me.

♘ Cassie and Charm ♘

Olivia just put her arm
around me and nodded,
and she didn't look like she
hated me or anything.

"I've been so wrapped up
in my own feelings about Apple, it seems like
I've been really horrible to people," I said then.
"But I haven't meant to be—honestly."

Olivia didn't say anything mean to me, but
instead just said, "Don't worry. It'll blow over."

"It won't!" I sobbed. "I don't even blame
them for not liking me. And Sally was right—I
haven't even given Charm a chance! I haven't
bothered to get to know him at all, or to
spend any time with him."

Olivia squeezed my shoulders and said,
"Well, turning your thinking around is the first
step to making changes! That's what Mom
always says, anyway. Now that you've done
that, everything should get easier."

I can't believe Olivia was still nice to me after how I've acted. She really is a cool girl. I know I've lost my chance to do the cross country, but at least I can still enjoy my week here, starting tomorrow. I'll be extra-friendly to the girls, and I'm going to try really, really hard with Charm.

Wednesday, almost time to go down to the yard—
and I've got butterflies in my tummy!

I'll tell you why in a minute!

Today is my brand-new start at Pony Camp, and it's been going well so far. At breakfast, when Yasmine was telling us about her riding stables, I listened to her carefully without any interrupting. I think she was surprised, but she seems happier to talk to me now, so that's good.

Then when it was cleaning up and brushing teeth time, Jess wanted someone to take the staff rotation to Sally, and I offered to do it. I wanted to talk to her on my own, even though my heart was pounding in case she got angry with me again. As I handed Sally the rotation, I said I was sorry for not giving Charm a chance, and I promised to try hard in her lessons.

She smiled. "Good girl, Cassie," she said. "And remember, enjoying Charm doesn't mean you're letting Apple down."

I hadn't realized it, but that's how I've been feeling, like if I have a good time with Charm, then I'm being mean to Apple. I sat down on the bench in the office, because suddenly my legs felt very wobbly. Sally sat next to me and put her arm around my shoulders. "Apple will always be with you in your heart and in your happy memories, but she wouldn't want you to stop riding, would she?" she said gently.

I couldn't say anything back because my throat felt all funny, but I managed to shake my head.

Then Sally said something amazing that I

wasn't expecting at all, which was, "I don't usually go back on my decisions, but this is a special case. Ride well this morning, and I'll think about letting you do the cross country after all."

How amazing is that?!

That's why I've got butterflies!

I'm going to work so hard with Charm in the lesson, and fingers crossed Sally will let us do the course.

I had a chance to say I was sorry to Charm, too, because this morning during yard duties, Sally said he looked a little muddy and asked me to give him a good groom. I spent a long time cleaning his face and combing his mane, while telling him all about Apple and how much I've been missing her.

"I'm so sorry for not making friends

with you before," I told him. He nudged my
arm and gave me a look, as if he understood.
Then I explained that we still had a chance to
do the cross country. He seemed excited, and
it's good that by spending time together, we've
started to become friends.

We're having our Pony Care lecture now,
which is called "All About Ponies," on markings
and breeds and conformation. If we do
anything in twos, I hope someone wants to go
with me today. I'm going to just smile and be
really nice, so hopefully they will!

Just quickly writing this before lunch

Jason called Sally away right after the lesson because someone was on the phone, so I don't know if I can do the cross country yet. The lesson went really well, but me and Charm didn't get everything right, so I'm not sure if Sally will say yes. Ugh! I'm so nervous, waiting to hear! I know—I'll write in here about the rest of the morning to try and take my mind off the suspense.

Me and Charm are even friendlier now. He's definitely beginning to like me (and he loves me ruffling his mane up!). I like him, too—he has beautiful dark eyes, which make it look like he's thinking important thoughts.

Things are going a little better with the other girls, too. When we were grooming and tacking up I helped Molly to pick out Sugar's feet, because she was a little nervous of him standing on her toes. But instead of taking over, I showed her how to lean into him a little and run her hand down his leg until he picked his hoof up. She was so proud when she did it all by herself. I'm not sure if Jordan saw. I really hope she did. Then she might stop thinking I'm a spoiled brat, and Ricosha and Tanika might be friendly to me again, too, because they tend to do what Jordan does and right now they are kind of half not talking to me.

In our Pony Care lecture, we had to go around the yard in twos, writing down the different markings on the ponies and guessing which breeds they might have in them. Olivia wasn't there because she's done all this before, and as soon as Lydia said get into pairs, Jordan grabbed Skye's hand. I tried not to mind and made myself keep smiling, and I was surprised

when Molly said she wanted to go with me
(and v. happy). When it was her turn with the
clipboard I spelled out some words for her,
but only when she asked me to.

In the lesson (my big test!) we warmed
up in walk and trot on each rein and did a
bunch of turns and circles to get our ponies
listening. We worked on getting a collected,
controlled canter with lots of impulsion for
the cross country. It's not as if me and Charm
were doing everything perfectly, but we were
definitely more of a team. Sally set up three
jumps, and we got over them, trying to look
ahead at the next one as we landed.

Sally kept calling out, "Look ahead and think ahead!" to everyone, which is her motto. (She's also always saying that we have to make sure we give our ponies the freedom of their head and necks as we go over the jumps.) I tried not to wonder what Sally was thinking of my riding. Instead, I just focused on working with Charm. Jordan got Mischief over the jumps after a couple of run outs, and everyone said great job. I said it the loudest and she smiled at me and my stomach flipped over and I started thinking that maybe everything will turn out okay after all. Oh, Sally's….

*　　*　　*

Yes, I can do the cross country! Yesssssssss!!! Sally said I had really tried and shown good improvement, although I've still got things to work on. Gotta go to lunch now. But I just want to quickly write again that I AM DOING THE CROSS COUNTRY—HOORAY!

The cross-country practice was amazing!!

I'm going to put down everything I did, but first I need to go back to where I left off and write about this afternoon so I don't leave anything out.

After lunch, instead of having a Pony Care lecture, our group went out with Sally and walked the cross-country course! Most of us had never done cross country before. We didn't have to decide our own route in and out of each jump, thank goodness! Instead, Sally showed us the best lines of approach. She also helped us line up the jumps with objects in the distance so we could make sure we were on the right track.

We were all really excited, but also a bit scared because the jumps look so solid that we were worried they'd hurt our ponies' legs if we didn't get over cleanly. Sally explained that fixed jumps are actually less scary to ponies because they can see them more easily. That means they tend to judge the take-off better and do a bigger jump (as I soon found out on Charm!). Luckily, the ground is pretty much flat, so we don't have to worry about going up or downhill, either—phew!

Skye walked the course with us, but she still wasn't sure about doing it. In the end she decided to try a few of the jumps with us today, and then think about whether to do the whole course and the competition after that.

Here is my pic of the course. I've written some of the helpful hints Sally gave us on it so I can remember what she said.

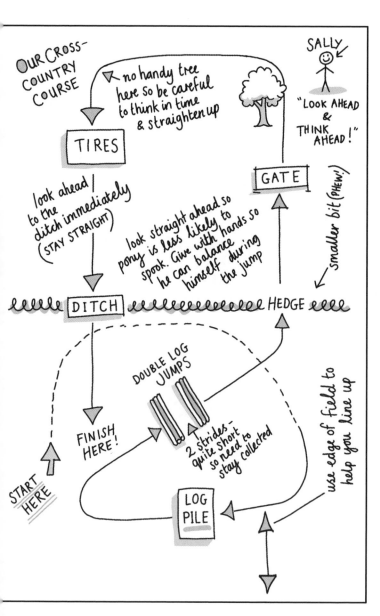

We were all buzzing with excitement as we went back to the yard to tack up our ponies and get ready for the cross-country practice. I was telling Charm all about the course while I did up his throatlatch and made sure his numnah was straight underneath his saddle. Of course, I know he couldn't understand exactly what I was saying, but he could tell we were in for some F★U̶N̶! His ears pricked up, and he started wandering out of the barn before I'd even gotten the reins over his head to lead him!

We all mounted in the yard and then rode into the manège to warm up. Charm's trot was bouncier than usual, and his canter was quicker off the leg. I think it was because I was listening to him more, so I knew when he needed a nudge, plus I had a much more relaxed contact so he wanted to work with me in the first place. I was surprised at how much better things were—I think I'm starting to see why

Charm is called Charm. Sally gave me a wink and a smile—she'd noticed the improvement, too! When she led us out of the manège and up to the field, my heart was thumping with excitement.

To start with, we all had a turn of going over the log, past the double, and back over the log again, just to get used to jumping out in the open. Skye was a little nervous at first, and Fisher lost confidence and ran out on their first try. When she got over on the second try, we all cheered, and Sally said, "See? It's as easy as jumping over a log—ha ha!"

Next we took a turn at the log and the double! Sally warned us that we had to keep calm and collected over the two brush fences as the strides in between are very short. Mischief rushed it and only put in one stride, and then he had to take a giant leap to get over the second half of the fence. We all gasped and squeezed our eyes shut, but they made it over—just! Sally told Jordan to circle him a couple of times to get a more collected canter and then bring him around again, and this time Jordan had more control, and he got the two strides in.

When it was my turn, I was thinking about what strides Charm was doing and when I should go into the jumping position, and I bobbed up too early. I had to grab onto his mane so I didn't go flying over his head! Sally told me to let the pony do the jumping and to "look ahead and think ahead." We were all smiling at each other when she said it. I tried again, but I still got my timing wrong.

Then we all jumped the hedge into the next field (which was really fun, because it was so soft, we weren't panicking about our ponies' hooves brushing it!). Charm loved it, and so did I. We flew over and as we came to a halt, I gave him a big pat to say good job.

Great job!

In the next field we jumped the gate and the spread fence, but we didn't add the ditch on. Sally said we'd tackle that on Friday morning because she didn't want us to do too much all at once. Even Skye enjoyed herself in the end, and she couldn't stop grinning when we were riding back to the yard. I really think she might do the competition after all!

When we got back to the barn, I grabbed a quick drink from the fountain and took my very hot hat off! Then I untacked Charm and spent a lot of time rubbing him and telling him how well he'd done. He seemed really proud of himself, and as he nuzzled my arm with his soft muzzle, I thought he was trying to let me know that he was proud of me, too—not just for the cross country, but for cheering up and trying hard.

I wish we could have another practice on the course tomorrow, but we've got our day trip out to the beach instead. That will be a ton of fun, though, and I'm totally looking forward to cantering on the sand with Charm. I just wish we had more time to work on our cross-country skills, too!

And we certainly need it—back in the yard, Sally gave us all helpful comments on our weak areas. I can't remember everything, but Jordan's was to keep control of Mischief's pace with half halts and by changing down into trot when he's getting too strong in canter.

Cassie and Charm

Ricosha's was to ride Flame more positively toward the jump so that she has less chance of refusing, and to look over to the other side of the jump rather than at it.

It was so funny when Sally turned to Olivia because Olivia knew exactly what she was going to say—"Keep Tally on course." He needs to stay focused after each jump because

he likes to tear off randomly across the field!

Then it was my turn. Sally said that I wasn't quite trusting Charm to clear the jump, how I was looking down instead of ahead sometimes and also going into the jumping position too early. She called it getting in front of the pony, which she says is a bad idea because it's very easy to come flying off that way! I've really got some catching up to do, but I'm glad I'm not the only one with things to work on.

She also said I need to concentrate on leading Charm instead of trying to do the jump for him. I knew what she meant, but it still made me giggle, imagining this!

When she'd given us all our comments, she said, "And one final thing for all of you to remember…" and we chanted, "Look ahead and think ahead!" and then burst into giggles! Sally grinned and said, "You're a silly bunch, but at least you're listening!"

I couldn't help grinning, too. It's so great to be one of the silly bunch again!

In bed

I've tried going to sleep (like Olivia and Skye), but I'm too excited about everything! So I turned on my flashlight, and I'm writing this under the covers instead.

Tonight, after me and Skye had done our dish-drying duty, we had another game night … but in the swimming pool this time! It was so funny—we had these relay races where you do different strokes, and then hopping and jogging, passing a float, throwing a ball to the next person, and things like that.

Jess put us into teams, and when she said, "Cassie, you're with Skye, Jordan, and Yasmine," it was really cool because Skye went, "Yes!" like she was really happy they were getting me, and Jordan smiled at me, too. Olivia's brother Tyler joined in to even out the numbers, and Ricosha and Tanika kept giggling about having a boy on their team. That was cool because it put them off a bit and we won the first two races! Hee hee!

Then they won two, and then it was the

final race—the tiebreaker.

When the last person on each team was on the way back, we all started cheering wildly. Molly was our last one, jogging through the water with the float, and we all cheered her on, and guess what…. We won! Jess said it was because we'd worked really well as a team. I just hope I can be a good team with Charm, too, so we trust each other more in the cross country. If we can do that, I still think we might have a chance to win.

I've got to put this diary down now, 'cos my eyes are closing on their own….

Thursday, after dinner

We had such a great time at the beach today! Before we left we had our Pony Care lecture about bandages for traveling. Lydia did a demo on Sparkle, then we all did the same on our ponies' legs and tails. It was really hard to get the tail bandage right—when Lydia inspected them, we were all laughing 'cos she just barely touched Molly's and it fell off Sugar's tail, and mine wasn't much better, either!

We didn't have space in the horse box to take all the ponies to the beach, so we had to double up and share. Sally brought her own horse, Blue, and she let Jordan ride him, too! Skye and me rode Charm (yay!), Ricosha and Tanika shared Flame, Olivia and Yasmine rode Prince, and Ruby and Molly rode Sugar.

I let Skye ride first, and she kept to the sand because Charm wasn't too comfortable in the water. But when it was my turn, with Sally helping me, I got him into the foamy waves. She told me to ride him forward and act like everything was fine, and after a couple of little nervous moments, he decided it must be okay if I thought so!

Soon we were playing that game where you wait for the waves, and then turn around and try to race away from them. I always play it with Henry on vacation in Maine, but it was a lot more fun on horseback. Charm loved it, too! He shook his head in delight as this one big wave crashed around his legs, and he looked so cute I just had to lean forward and give him a big hug!

After that, me, Olivia, and Tanika had a canter up the beach with Sally, and she showed us how to get a lot of impulsion without getting the ponies too excited. I think I've finally gotten the hang of half halts now

and how to squeeze Charm forward with
my leg so he has more energy in the canter
instead of just getting faster. He's certainly not
going along with his nose poking out anymore!

Later on, Sally found these two pieces of
driftwood and set them up as jumps. Flame
wouldn't take Tanika over on her own, so
Sally gave her a lead, and they went flying
over! Then we all wanted to try giving leads,
so we kept going over in pairs in different
combinations. I went with Olivia, then with
Tan, then Sally, and afterward I just couldn't
stop grinning! Then we changed places and
Jordan, Skye, and Ricosha had a few turns over
the jumps, too, and we all cheered for them.

The trip was so great that I didn't want it
to end! On the van home, we were all singing
songs and giggling about girly stuff, like
Jordan liking this boy in her town. Sally came
and chatted with us, too, and when everyone

else was busy singing, she asked how I was.

That's when I realized I'd been so caught up in the fun I'd hardly missed Apple all day. And I said, "I feel great! I wanted to practice on the cross-country course today, but it's actually lucky that we came to the beach, because I got the chance to get Charm to trust me about splashing in the waves, and I know how to get a collected canter now and he jumped that driftwood even better than the logs on the course!" Sally did a mysterious kind of smile and said, "Yeah, that was lucky. I hadn't planned it at all!" and I knew she meant that she had! She's such an amazing teacher, and so is Charm. We're really turning into a team now!

Oh, gotta go—it's time for our movie night (with popcorn—yum!). We're going to watch this one about the Horse Trials and get some inspiration for the cross-country comp tomorrow!

♘ Cassie and Charm ♘

Friday morning, and I've just woken up

It's cross-country day—hooray!! But also our last day at Pony Camp—boo!!

The movie we saw last night was amazing. The fences were HUGE! We were all going "Oooh!" and "Ahhhh!" watching the horses and riders go over them, and "Eeeeeekkkk!" and "Wow!" when they were jumping the really tricky ones like the coffin. We're even more excited about getting out onto the cross-country course after seeing that!

Skye, Olivia, and me had planned to stay up and have a midnight feast because it was our last night here (well, mine and Skye's, anyway), but we all fell asleep by accident! I just remembered I had a really weird dream about Apple. We were on a beach and I was cantering along

Zzzzzz

on her, and then suddenly I was on Charm instead and Apple was standing with Laura, the girl who bought her. Somehow I just knew Apple was happy, and I felt happy for her. When I woke up I still felt that way, too! Of

 course I'll always miss Apple, but I'm sure she's having fun with Laura, and I guess it's nicer to have an owner the right size to ride you, so that you can have a lot of adventures together.

I've got to get dressed now because we're having another lesson on the cross-country course this morning, and then getting our ponies ready for the comp!

I can't wait!!!

Still Friday!

I'm back at home. I've had a shower, and I'm in my pajamas—Mom couldn't believe it when I said I wanted to go to bed early! Really I wanted to come up to my room and finish off my Pony Camp Diary before I forget one single thing about my amazing day!

For our morning lesson, we warmed up in the manège and then went out to practice on the cross-country course. Sally asked me to give Skye a lead over the log to get her started on a good note. I was so proud that she'd chosen me and Charm to lead someone else over a jump! And I could tell that Charm was pleased with himself, too! After jumping in pairs on the beach yesterday we just flew over, and Skye and Fisher followed with no worries.

Everyone was much less nervous and giggly than the first time we came out onto the course, probably because the beach ride had given us more confidence. Plus, it wasn't as hot today, so we weren't absolutely boiling in our body protectors and long sleeves and hats and everything! We did the course in two parts— first we took a turn at the log pile, the double, and the hedge, and then when we were all in the next field, we tried the gate, tire jump, and....

Yes, we finally tackled the ditch!

The water looked a little SPOOKY! because the bank on either side was really grassy and there were bushes hanging over it, which made strange reflections. But after getting Charm into the waves, I knew that he would trust me around spooky-looking water, as long as I acted like it was fine. In fact, I stayed so calm and confident, and Charm was so into his stride after the tire jump, that he didn't even think about stopping at the ditch and just popped right over it!

Once Skye had seen us clearing it, she decided to try it, too. It was a little messy, with Fisher putting the brakes on, and then doing a huge leap so she had to really hang on, but at least they got over! Sally said, "Well, now that you've done the ditch and both halves of the course, you might as well go for the competition this afternoon. But, of course, you don't have to if you don't feel like it...."

"I'd like to," Skye said shyly, and we all cheered for her. "But I'm telling you now that I'm probably going to come in last," she added.

We all started saying how it was just for fun and it didn't matter who finished where. Sally laughed and said, "Well, I was about to say that myself, but you girls have said it for me. I've taught you everything you need to know. I might as well go home!"

Ricosha didn't realize she was joking and cried, "Oh, no, don't! We need you!" and that made everyone else laugh, too.

Sally also said we could do up our ponies for the cross country however we liked, as long as they were well groomed and neat, and it didn't have to be all proper like the official Pony Club comps or anything. I got really creative with Charm and did a running braid in his mane with blue ribbons in it, and gave him

heart-shaped quarter marks
using a stencil and
some hairspray.

We all cleaned our
tack until it gleamed,
and then got into our
best gear. I'd saved my
cream jodhs especially
for the comp, and
my pink striped top
had the least mud on it
so I wore that, too, with my body protector
underneath. My pink silk almost matches it,
and with that and my long boots on, I felt like
a real cross-country rider! I felt even more like
one when Jess gave us numbers to pin onto
our tops. No one else wanted to go last and
I said I didn't mind, so I was number 6!

Just as the parents started arriving, Sally
gathered us around in the yard and explained

the scoring system, which is like this:

First refusal—4 penalty points

2nd refusal—8 penalty points

3rd refusal—elimination

Knocking the gate down—4 penalty points

Fall of pony—elimination

Fall of rider—8 penalty points

2nd fall of rider—elimination

I was so excited when our car pulled up and Mom and Dad and Henry spilled out. Mom had told me she'd be coming on her own, so it was awesome to see them all! Dad said, "A little bird gave us a call last night and said how well you were doing, so I took the day off from work, and we picked up Henry on the way. We can't wait to see you in action, Cassie!" I gave them all hugs (even my annoying big bro!). It was great seeing how proud they were of me before they'd even watched me ride one single step! And by the way, I found out later that the little bird was Sally!

When all of the parents had arrived, we mounted up and rode out to the field. I was feeling very nervous, and Charm picked up on that and began prancing around, so I sat deep in my saddle, slowed my breathing

calm

down, and relaxed through my shoulders and arms. It made me feel much better, and Charm soon settled down, too!

After the warm-up and a practice jump each, it was time for the comp. The moms and dads, and Group A, and Lydia and Jess and Tyler all leaned on the fence beside the ditch so that they could still see us when we jumped the hedge.

This is how we did:

Ricosha + Flame

Ricosha had a refusal at the log pile, so it wasn't a great start. But she got it together, and they flew around the rest of the course with no problems! *4 penalty points.*

Jordan + Mischief

Mischief ran out at the gate— twice! Jordan managed to get him over on the third try, so she didn't get eliminated, but she kept giggling, which didn't exactly help. And after the ditch Mischief did another lap around the field because he didn't want to stop! *12 penalty points!!*

Tanika + Sparkle

Those two did great until … Tan fell off over the tires! Sparkle stopped suddenly, then did a big leap and sent

Tan flying over her head. We all went **GASP!** like we did when we were watching the Horse Trials, but amazingly, Tan was fine, and she got back on and finished the course. Go, girl! *8 penalty points.*

Olivia + Tally

Those two got eliminated for going the wrong way! Sally shouted, "Olivia, how many times have you done this course?" Olivia was grinning, going, "I know, but it wasn't me who decided to race over to the other side of the field!" I don't think Tally is ever going to win her any prizes, but she loves him all the same! *Eliminated (whoops!).*

Skye + Fisher

Skye took it really slow and steady, going into trot between jumps, and if only they hadn't had the gate down, they would have gone clear. But it *was* very fragile! She got a little flustered after that, but we all cheered her on, and she collected her reins and trotted a circle around the tree before taking off toward the tire jump. Fisher flew over that *and* the ditch, and when they came to a stop, Skye was absolutely beaming! She kept saying she just couldn't believe they'd jumped the whole course. Especially when at the beginning of the week she never even thought she'd come out here! *4 penalty points (they did great!).*

And what about me?

Well, I wish I could write that I had ZERO faults and I WON, but that would be a BIG FIB!!

Charm went like a dream over the log pile, and we got a great straight central approach over the double. We turned late after that (my fault— I was too busy thinking PHEW! about us

getting over the double without knocking
the second half down). Thank goodness the
hedge was next so we could brush through
it. If it had been the gate, we'd definitely have
knocked it down. I pulled myself together
then and looked ahead, past the gate, and
Charm just got on and jumped it without me
"helping" (ahem!).

Then we romped around
the tree in a balanced
canter, like the one we
had going on the beach
ride. We were nicely lined
up for the tire jump, but for
some reason, Charm put in an extra stride at
the last minute and jumped a really long way
over it, so we weren't quite right for the ditch,
and he just suddenly stopped in front of it.

The crowd at the fence all gasped as I
almost went flying over his neck, but I managed

to barely hold on! My heart was pounding—
we'd flown over the ditch in the morning
lesson, so I just hadn't been expecting a refusal!
But I shook off my disappointment and circled
Charm around again.

Looking back now, I know what I did wrong
on my second turn, but I didn't realize it at the
time. I tried to take charge and bobbed up too
soon, just the thing Sally had warned me not
to do! It unbalanced Charm and he clattered
to a stop in front of the ditch again. One more
refusal and we'd be eliminated.

I was about to get really frustrated, but then
I stopped myself. After all, me and Charm
were a team, and we weren't going to fall
apart at the last hurdle (and it actually was the
last hurdle—hee hee!). I imagined us jumping
the driftwood on the beach and tried to feel
like I had felt then. The thought made me
smile, and when I relaxed, Charm did, too.

♞ Cassie and Charm ♞

I trotted on, rode a circle, and picked up canter as I turned in front of the tire jump. I kept Charm really collected so we'd have a lot of impulsion and he'd know that we could easily clear the ditch. I looked up and ahead like it was no big deal, gave Charm a

final squeeze to urge him on … and then we were landing. We were over! Instead of sitting forward too soon, I'd just  naturally left my seat and hinged at the hips at the right time without even thinking about it. I had felt like I was part of the movement. Like I was part of Charm!

So in the end I had 12 faults, the same as Jordan, meaning that we came in tied for last, except for Olivia!!

Oh, well, it's okay!!

We all got rosettes, though, so I've still got something to put on my wall! Mom took pix of us all after the awards ceremony, but I haven't printed them out yet, so here's my drawing:

Ricosha   Tanika   me!   Skye   Jordan   Olivia

When Sally presented me with my rosette, Mom and Dad were clapping and cheering just as much as if I'd come in first! I didn't really mind being second to last—especially because Jordan put her arm through mine and called out, "We're tied for last! Take a bow, Cassie!" We both took a bow at the same time, and everyone laughed and clapped for us. We were giggling and I said, "I can't believe it! I really thought you'd win!"

Jordan's eyes widened and she said, "Did you? I really thought you would!"

After we'd taken our ponies back to the barn and untacked them, we got drinks and watched Group A playing their gymkhana games. It was a lot of fun clapping and cheering for them, and when the last race came around, I didn't want it to end! Soon it was time to bring our stuff downstairs. We went into the older girls' room to exchange addresses, and all nine of us ended up piling together in a special Pony Camp hug! When Sally came up to see where we'd gone, we'd toppled over and were lying on the floor in total hysterics!

Skye held up her rosette and said to Sally, "I still can't believe it!"

Sally grinned. "You did it one step at a time, and that's all it takes! Isn't that right, Cassie?"

I sat up and gave her a puzzled look. I didn't know what she was talking about at first. But then I realized she meant that I'd gotten over Apple by just taking one step at a time.

Getting back into a yard and joining in with the girls was one step, and so was making friends with Charm. Trying the cross country was another step, and our teamwork on the beach ride was a step, too. And finally, trusting each other to tackle that ditch was a big step (well, a giant leap, actually!).

It was so hard to say good-bye to the girls, and even when we'd brought our stuff down, we kept hugging and taking pictures and then hugging more, until Ricosha's mom said she really had to get going because it's a long way to Charleston. It was time to say good-bye to the ponies, too (boo hoo!).

I made a great big fuss of Charm, my fabulous pony for the week, and told him how wonderful he was. Also, I told him again that I was sorry for being such a grouch at the start of Pony Camp and whispered about 24 thank yous in his ear for teaching me so much.

Of course, I'll never forget Apple, but thanks to Charm, I'm ready to start riding some of the beautiful ponies at my stables. If I start going to the lessons again, I'll get to hang around the yard and help out with the other girls, too. I might even enter our local cross-country comp, because now that I've done it once, I don't want to stop! I could ask to take Frosty from the stables, or maybe my friend Mara would lend me her dapple gray, Storm. And who knows—maybe one day, if I'm lucky, I'll even get another pony of my own!

So, thank you, Sunnyside, and thank you, Charm!

Cassie xxx

PONY CAMP
diaries

Learn all about
the world of ponies!

Glossary

Bending—directing the horse to ride correctly around a curve

Bit—the piece of metal that goes inside the horse's mouth. Part of the bridle.

Chase Me Charlie—a show jumping game where the jumps get higher and higher

Currycomb—a comb with rows of metal teeth used to clean (to curry) a pony's coat

Dandy brush—a brush with hard bristles that removes the dirt, hair, and any other debris stirred up by the currycomb

Frog—the triangular soft part on the underside of the horse's hoof. It's very important to clean around it with a hoof pick.

Girth—the band attached to the saddle and buckled around the horse's barrel to keep the saddle in place

Grooming—the daily cleaning and caring for the horse to keep them healthy and make them beautiful for competitions. A full grooming includes brushing your horse's coat, mane, and tail and picking out the hooves.

Gymkhana—a fun event full of races and other competitions

Hands—a way to measure the height of a horse

Glossary

Mane—the long hair on the back of a horse's neck. Perfect for braiding!

Manège—an enclosed training area for horses and their riders

Numnah—a piece of material that lies under the saddle and stops it from rubbing against the horse's back

Paces—a horse has four main paces, each made up of an evenly repeated sequence of steps. From slowest to quickest, these are the walk, trot, canter, and gallop.

Plodder—a slow, reliable horse

Pommel—the raised part at the front of the saddle

Pony—a horse under 14.2 hands in height

Rosette—a rose-shaped decoration with ribbons awarded as a prize! Usually, a certain color matches where you are placed during the competition.

Stirrups—foot supports attached to the sides of a horse's saddle

Tack—the main pieces of the horse's equipment, including the saddle and bridle. Tacking up a horse means getting them ready for riding.

Pony Colors

*Ponies come in all **colors**. These are some of the most common!*

Bay—Bay ponies have rich brown bodies and black manes, tails, and legs.

Black—A true black pony will have no brown hairs, and the black can be so pure that it looks a bit blue!

Chestnut—Chestnut ponies have reddish-brown coats that vary from light to dark red with no black points.

Dun—A dun pony has a sandy-colored body, with a black mane, tail, and legs.

Gray—Gray ponies come in a range of color varieties, including dapple gray, steel gray, and rose gray. They all have black skin with white, gray, or black hair on top.

Palomino—Palominos have a sandy-colored body with a white or cream mane and tail. Their coats can range from pale yellow to bright gold!

Piebald—Piebald ponies have a mixture of black-and-white patches—like a cow!

Skewbald—Skewbald ponies have patches of white and brown.

Pony Markings

*As well as the main body color, many ponies also have white **markings** on their faces and legs!*

On the legs:

Socks—run up above the fetlock but lower than the knee. The fetlock is the joint several inches above the hoof.

Stockings—extend to at least the bottom of the horse's knee, sometimes higher

On the face:

Blaze—a wide, straight stripe down the face from in between the eyes to the muzzle

Snip—a white marking on the horse's muzzle, between the nostrils

Star—a white marking between the eyes

Stripe—the same as a blaze but narrower

White/bald face—a very wide blaze that goes out past the eyes, making most of the horse's face look white!

Fan-tack-stic Cleaning Tips!

*Get your **tack** shining in no time with these top tips!*

- Clean your tack after every use, if you can. Otherwise, make sure you at least rinse the bit under running water and wash off any mud or sweat from your girth after each ride.

- The main things you will need are:
  — bars of saddle soap
  — a soft cloth
  — a sponge
  — a bottle of leather conditioner

- As you clean your bit, check that it has no sharp edges and isn't too worn.

- Use a bridle hook or saddle horse to hold your bridle and saddle as you clean them. If you don't have a saddle horse, you can hang a blanket over a gate to put the saddle on. Avoid hanging your bridle on a single hook or nail because the leather might crack!

- Make sure you look carefully at the bridle before undoing it so that you know how to put it back together!
- Use the conditioner to polish the leather of the bridle and saddle and make them sparkle!
- Check under your numnah before you clean it. If the dirt isn't evenly spread on both sides, you might not be sitting evenly as you ride.
- Polish your metalwork occasionally. Cover the leather parts around it with a cloth and only polish the rings—not the mouthpiece, because that would taste horrible!

Going the Distance!

Find out how much you know about cross-country riding with this fun quiz! Can you go the distance?

1. For safety, the rider must wear:
 a. A body warmer
 b. A body protector
 c. Full body armor

2. Cross-country boots can be worn by your pony to:
 a. Look stylish
 b. Make them go faster
 c. Protect their legs from knocks

3. "Narrow," "angled," and "corner" are all types of:
 a. Events
 b. Fences
 c. Ditches

4. Cross-country riding differs from racing, as your pony should never finish:
 a. Exhausted
 b. Hungry
 c. Angry

5. Cross country forms part of three day eventing competitions, along with:
   a.   Showjumping and racing
   b.   Showjumping and dressage
   c.   Dressage and dressing-up

6. A cross-country rider usually wears a:
   a.   Skull cap
   b.   Skeleton cap
   c.   Shower cap

7. All cross-country courses are designed to:
   a.   Look the same
   b.   Look different
   c.   Look exciting but a little scary

8. An advanced water combination includes a number of:
   a.   Riders and routes
   b.   Riders and fences
   c.   Fences and routes

❧ Beautiful Braids! ❧

Follow this step-by-step guide to give your pony a perfect tail braid!

1. Start at the very top of the tail and take two thin bunches of hair from either side, braiding them into a strand in the center.

2. Continue to pull in bunches from either side and braid down the center of the tail.

3. Keep braiding like this, making sure you're pulling the hair tightly to keep the braid from unraveling!

4. When you reach the end of the dock—where the bone ends—stop taking in bunches from the side but keep braiding downward until you run out of hair.

5. Fasten with a braid band!

Gymkhana Ready!

Get your pony looking spectacular for the gymkhana with these grooming ideas!

A running MANE BRAID

Ribbons on her brow band

Matching ribbons in tail braid

POLISHED coat

HOOF oil & Sequins on hooves

Turn the page for a sneak peek
at the next story in the series!

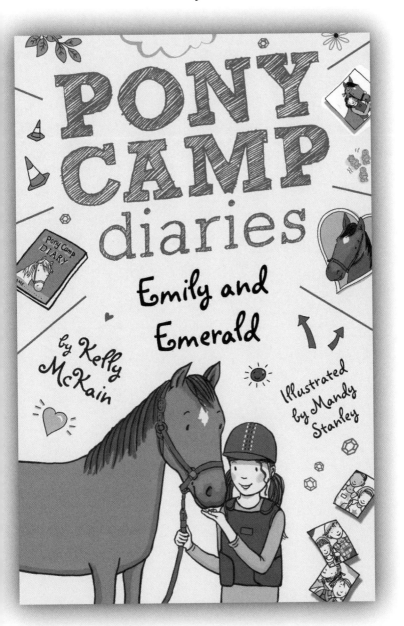

PONY CAMP diaries

Emily and Emerald

by Kelly McKain

Illustrated by Mandy Stanley

Monday—I can't believe I'm really here at Pony Camp!

I feel EXCITED about being here, but NERVOUS at the same time!

I'm EXCITED 'cos I haven't ridden since we moved here from Philadelphia three weeks ago —I can't wait to get back in the saddle! And I'm NERVOUS because at the stables where I used to ride and help out on weekends, there were these older girls and … well, I don't really want to write all about what happened with them in my beautiful new Pony Camp Diary. And, anyway, this is meant to be a new beginning.

Actually, me and Mom are both getting a fresh start down here in Milton. Since it's summer vacation, I haven't started at my new school yet, so it's been a bit boring 'cos I've just been helping Mom unpack boxes and paint the living room.

I felt extra NERVOUS when Jess showed us up here to my room. I wanted Mom to stay for a while, but she had to go back to the new house and wait for the electrician, so I ended up on my own. There are three beds in here, and Jess said the one by the window was her daughter Olivia's, so I had the choice out of the bunk beds. I went for the bottom one, and as I started unpacking my stuff, I could hear all this noise and laughter coming from the room next door.

The two girls in there were really loud and confident—the exact opposite of ME! Then I heard all these footsteps on the stairs and someone yelling, "Hey, Charlie!" at the top of their voice. For one second I thought there was a BOY at Pony Camp, but then I heard this girl's voice yelling back, and I realized that Charlie must be short for Charlotte.

And that was when Frankie bustled in with her mom, who is also really loud and who kept on calling her Francesca. I felt really shy and I wished I could shrink into a corner and disappear. But when Frankie rolled her eyes at me, I couldn't help smiling. She shooed her mom out and said hello, and after a few seconds of me blushing shyly with no words coming out, I finally managed to mumble, "Hi, I'm Emily."

Frankie said, "Hi, Ems. Call me Frankie—everyone does. Well, except for her, of course!"

She waved toward the door, obviously meaning her mom. "And my big sister Charlie when she's trying to annoy me! That's her loud voice you can hear, by the way—she has such a big mouth!"

I smiled as she threw her stuff on the top bunk. No one's ever called me Ems before—I really like it. I was trying to think of something to say when Charlie put her head around the door and shouted, "Come on, Frog Face, we're all going down to the yard!"

She grabbed Frankie's arm and started pulling her out of the room. Frankie giggled and cried, "Don't call me Frog Face, Monkey Breath!" Then Frankie tried to grab my arm, and I wanted to go with them, but my feet stayed stuck to the spot. For some reason, I don't seem to be that good at joining in.

"I'll be down in a sec!" I told them as brightly as I could. "I just want to start off my diary first."

So that's what I've been doing!

Oh, hang on, even the other room with the younger girls in it is quiet, so everyone must be outside. Okay, I'm going to take a deep breath and put on my hat and body protector (and a big smile) and go down to the yard.

Monday 1:45 p.m.—well, I
still can't believe what happened
this morning!

I'm so EXCITED and NERVOUS again!
EXCITED because I have met the most amazing
pony named Emerald, who I'm desperate to
have as my own for the week. And NERVOUS
because I'm waiting to hear from Sally, our
instructor, about whether I can have her or not.

Sally went to speak to Jason about it (he's
the yard manager and also Olivia's dad), and she
said she'll come and find me after lunch. We've
finished eating now, and I'm writing this sitting at
the picnic table outside the farmhouse so I can
keep a lookout for her.

Okay, well, this is a pic of (fingers crossed!)
my fabulous pony, Emerald!

She isn't supposed to be one of the Pony
Camp ponies at all, but as soon as I saw her

Emerald

I knew I wanted her, and Sally did admit it seems like Emerald has chosen me, too. But she also said I'd have to ride Flame first in the assessment and, whoops, I'm trying to say everything at once and messing things up. Okay, I'll take a deep breath and slow down and write everything in order.

So I headed over to the yard to find the others, and as I walked between the parking lot and lower field, this pony came bolting toward me, completely loose, with a head collar on and her lead rope dangling. It was Emerald!

I didn't know her name then, of course. And I didn't know that she'd just arrived at Sunnyside and had bolted out of the trailer as Sally was unloading her. But I did know that she was the most beautiful pony I'd ever seen.

She was skittering around, looking really scared. For a moment I froze in shock, but then I thought how dangerous that dangling lead rope was, and how I had to stop her from tripping on it and having an accident.

I stood my ground as she came right up to me, and I spread my arms out so that she couldn't get past and gallop off up the track to the upper fields.

I took a deep breath and tried to relax. Emerald lowered her head and snorted; she seemed to be calming down a bit, too. I stepped toward her and put my hand out for her to smell.

"Be careful!" Sally called as she appeared around the corner. I gave a slight nod, then slowly turned so I was standing at Emerald's shoulder and reached down for the end of the lead rope. Then I stood there with both hands on the rope while Sally came over and took it from me. "Great job!" she said softly. "You showed a lot of horse sense by staying so calm."

I smiled, and inside I was really proud of myself.

She asked my name, and just when I thought she was going to send me off to the yard to join the others, she said I could help take Emerald into the barn instead. She told me to lead her into a small pen in the corner, away from the other ponies. As I walked her, I kept glancing at her shiny, glossy bay coat and cute white star and big brown eyes and thinking how beautiful and special she was.

We got some hay for her and filled up her water trough, and as I was rubbing her nose to say good-bye, I blurted out to Sally, "Do you think maybe I could have Emerald as my pony this week?"

Sally frowned. "I'm sorry, Emily, but she's not going to be ridden at Pony Camp for a while," she said. "She's very nervous, and I need to work with her myself first."

I tried to smile, but I couldn't hide how disappointed I was. Emerald leaned her head over the railing and nudged my arm. I rubbed her neck, and she snorted gently.

"It wouldn't be an easy week," Sally said then. I stared at her. Was she saying yes after all?

If you love animals, check out these series, too!

Pet Rescue Adventures

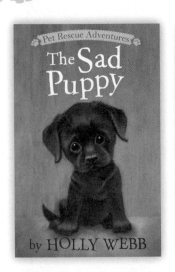

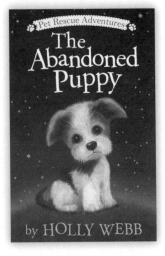

ANIMAL
RESCUE CENTER

ANIMAL
RESCUE CENTER

The
Abandoned
Hamster

by TINA NOLAN

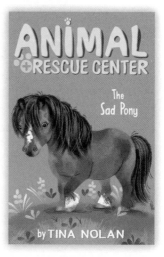

ANIMAL
RESCUE CENTER

The
Sad Pony

by TINA NOLAN

ANIMAL
RESCUE CENTER

The
Homeless
Foal

by TINA NOLAN

ANIMAL
RESCUE CENTER

The
Porch
Puppy

by TINA NOLAN

Kelly McKain

Kelly McKain is a best-selling children's and YA author with more than 40 books published in more than 20 languages. She lives in the beautiful Surrey Heath area of the UK with her family and loves horses, dancing, yoga, singing, walking, and being in nature. She came up with the idea for the Pony Camp Diaries while she was helping young riders at a summer camp, just like the one at Sunnyside Stables! She enjoys hanging out at the Holistic Horse and Pony Center, where she plays with and rides cute Smartie and practices her natural horsemanship skills with the Quantum Savvy group. Her dream is to do some bareback, bridleless jumping like New Zealand Free Riding ace Alycia Burton, but she has a ways to go yet!